Give your child a head start with
PICTURE READERS

Dear Parent,

Now children as young as preschool age can have the fun and satisfaction of reading a book all on their own.

In every Picture Reader, there are simple words, rebus pictures, and 24 flash cards to cut out and keep. (There is a flash card for every rebus picture plus extra cards for reading practice.) After children listen to each story a couple of times, they will be ready to try it all by themselves.

Collect all the titles in our Picture Reader series. Once children have mastered these books, they can move on to Levels 1, 2, and 3 in our All Aboard Reading series.

ISBN 0-448-41304-3   C D E F G H I J

A PICTURE READER

Lots of Hearts

By Maryann Cocca-Leffler

Grosset & Dunlap • New York

I am making  .

I have  ,

 , and .

My  wags

her .

She wants to help.

But I say no.

I make lots of .

I make a

for my dad.

It has a pink

and red  on it.

I hide it

in his .

I make a

for my mom.

It has a red

and pink

on it.

I hide it

in her .

I make a

for my .

It has a blue

and a yellow

on it.

I it

to the .

And I make a

for my .

It has a green

and a big  on it.

I hide it

in her .

Now I say to Dad,

"Look in your  .

You will find a  ."

Dad looks.

But there is

no  !

I say to Mom,

"Look in your  .

You will find a ."

Mom looks.

But there is

no  !

I go to

the  .

There is no

for the !

I go to the  .

Here are the  !

My has all

the  !

And my  also

has a big surprise

for me!

My  had !

What a happy

Valentine's Day!